Date: 01/30/12

J 508.2 SCH
Schuette, Sarah L.,
Let's look at winter /

Investigate the Seasons
Let's Look at Winter

by Sarah L. Schuette

Consulting Editor: Gail Saunders-Smith, PhD

Capstone
press®

Mankato, Minnesota

Pebble Plus is published by Capstone Press,
151 Good Counsel Drive, P.O. Box 669, Mankato, Minnesota 56002.
www.capstonepub.com

Library of Congress Cataloging-in-Publication Data
Schuette, Sarah L., 1976–
Let's look at winter / by Sarah L. Schuette.
   p. cm.—(Pebble plus. Investigate the seasons)
   Summary: "Simple text and photographs present what happens to the weather, animals, and plants in
winter"—Provided by publisher.
   Includes bibliographical references and index.
   ISBN-13: 978-0-7368-6706-1 (hardcover)
   ISBN-10: 0-7368-6706-6 (hardcover)
   1. Animal behavior—Juvenile literature. 2. Winter—Juvenile literature. I. Title. II. Series.
QL753.S384 2007
508.2—dc22   2006020508

Editorial Credits

Martha E. H. Rustad, editor; Bobbi J. Wyss, set designer; Veronica Bianchini, book designer; Kara Birr,
    photo researcher; Scott Thoms, photo editor

Photo Credits

Corbis/Donna Disario, cover (background tree)
Getty Images Inc./The Image Bank/Joseph Van Os, 12–13; The Image Bank/LWA, 5
iStockphoto Inc./Jonathan Clark, 19
Peter Arnold/Angelika Jakob, 20–21
Shutterstock/bora ucak, cover, 1 (magnifying glass); Doxa, 9; Ilya D. Gridnev, cover (inset leaf); Jeff Thrower
    (WebThrower), 16–17; Tim Elliott, 11; Tony Campbell, 15
SuperStock/age fotostock, 1 (snowballs); Tom Benoit, 7

The author dedicates this book to her friend Elizabeth Haugen Todd of Hutchinson, Minnesota.

Note to Parents and Teachers

The Investigate the Seasons set supports national science standards related to weather
and climate. This book describes and illustrates winter. The images support early readers
in understanding the text. The repetition of words and phrases helps early readers learn
new words. This book also introduces early readers to subject-specific vocabulary words,
which are defined in the Glossary section. Early readers may need assistance to read
some words and to use the Table of Contents, Glossary, Read More, Internet Sites, and
Index sections of the book.

Table of Contents

It's Winter!

How do you know it's winter?

The temperature is cold.

The ground hardens.

Water freezes.

When snow falls,

it covers everything.

The sun rises later
in the morning.
Winter days are
the shortest of the year.

Animals in Winter

What do animals do
in winter?
Deer search for food
under the snow.

Brown rabbits turn white.
Now their fur blends in
with the snow.

Cardinals sit

in evergreen trees.

They stay

for the whole winter.

Some birds migrate.

Plants in Winter

What happens
to plants in winter?
They do not grow.
Many plants look bare
and brown.

Evergreen trees stay green.

They keep their needles

all year round.

What's Next?

The temperature gets warmer.

Winter is over.

What season is next?

Glossary

bare—not covered

evergreen—a tree or bush that has green needles all year long

freeze—to become solid or icy at a very low temperature

migrate—to move from one place to another when seasons change

needle—a sharp, green leaf on an evergreen tree

season—one of the four parts of the year; winter, spring, summer, and fall are seasons.

temperature—the measure of how hot or cold something is

Read More

Davis, Rebecca Fjelland. *Snowflakes and Ice Skates: A Winter Counting Book.* Counting Books. Mankato, Minn.: Capstone Press, 2006.

Macken, JoAnn Early. *Winter.* Seasons of the Year. Milwaukee: Weekly Reader Early Learning Library, 2006.

Rustad, Martha E. H. *Today Is Snowy.* How's the Weather? Mankato, Minn.: Capstone Press, 2006.

Internet Sites

FactHound offers a safe, fun way to find Internet sites related to this book. All of the sites on FactHound have been researched by our staff.

Here's how:

1. Visit *www.facthound.com*

2. Choose your grade level.

3. Type in this book ID **0736867066** for age-appropriate sites. You may also browse subjects by clicking on letters, or by clicking on pictures and words.

4. Click on the **Fetch It** button.

FactHound will fetch the best sites for you!

Index

Word Count: 113
Grade: 1
Early Intervention Level: 13